The Other Side of the Story

of the Story

Fairy Tales with a Twist

PICTURE WINDOW BOOKS

a capstone imprint

The Other Side of the Story

Fairy Tales
with a
Twist

TABLE OF CONTENTS

No Kidding, Mermaids Are a Joke!
THE STORY OF
THE LITTLE MERMAID
as Told by the Prince

Believe Me, Goldilocks Rocks!
THE STORY OF
THE THREE BEARS
as Told by Baby Bear

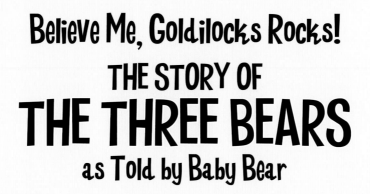

Honestly, Red Riding Hood Was Rotten!
THE STORY OF
LITTLE RED RIDING HOOD
as Told by the Wolf

Seriously, CINDERELLA IS SO ANNOYING!

The Story of
CINDERELLA
as Told by THE WICKED STEPMOTHER

by **Trisha Speed Shaskan**
illustrated by **Gerald Guerlais**

You must have heard of me. The *wicked* stepmother?
Not true. It's just another one of Cinderella's wild
stories. Not as wild as the one about the pumpkin.
And the fairy godmother. The *real* story, the *true*
story, began with some chatter—and some dust.

All I ever wanted was a husband and a mansion. Before I married Cindy's father, my two darlings and I had met Cindy only a few times. The girl had _seemed_ normal then.

After I married Cindy's father, my darlings and I moved in. When I had just one foot on the front step, my dear husband kissed me good-bye and said, "I'm off on business!"

"He leaves often," Cindy said, "but the animals stay put. They talk. They joke. They sing. They even help out—especially the bluebirds."

Now, I don't mind a story. But I like facts, not fiction.
Soon the girl was talking all kinds of hokey-pokey.

"Once upon a time," Cindy said, "one of the bluebirds
became blue. Not the color. The feeling. His friend had
flown south ..."

My darlings and I were stuck near the front door.
I just wanted to put away my bags. And that's when
I saw it: dust.

"Dear, is the whole house this dusty?" I asked.

"I don't know," Cindy said. "I'll give you a tour!"

In the dining room,
Cindy told stories.

In the study, Cindy told stories.

Nonstop.

"Girls," I said, "time to get to work. This place needs a good cleaning."

"Once upon a time, when I was cleaning ..." Cindy started.

Oh, boy.

Cindy mopped the floor. But she finished so fast!
My darlings had barely started.

"Did you know robins and sparrows are my friends?"
she said. "But the sparrows don't like the robins.
Silly creatures! Once upon a time, one of the
robins—"

"Cindy, dear," I said, "why don't you go and wash the
clothes now, hmm?"

But Cindy washed them so fast! How on earth did she do it? I had to find another chore for her, just to keep her busy.

"If there's one thing squirrels love, it's washing clothes," Cindy said. "The rats, though, would rather iron. You know, one day I—"

"Squirrels and rats doing laundry? Quit telling such foolish stories!" I said.

Time passed, but nothing changed.

In the garden, Cindy
told stories.

In the kitchen, Cindy told stories.

At dinner, I couldn't hear myself think.
"Dear, please," I said,

"STOP TALKING!"

But Cindy didn't stop.

One day, a letter arrived. It was an invitation to the king's ball. The prince would surely fall in love with one of my darlings. Then they would marry, live in a beautiful castle, and one day be king and queen of all the land!

"Oh, Stepmother, I have to go too!" said Cindy. "Once upon a time, a girl and a prince …"

And then—just like that—Cindy lost her voice. Imagine! It had to be from all that storytelling.

Well, what could I do? I told Cindy she had to stay home—for her health. She cried, of course. But a ball was no place for a sick girl. She needed rest.

Sometimes, it's so hard being a stepmother.

At the ball, my darlings twirled. They whirled.

But then some strange girl waltzed in.
Her gown was magnificent. I couldn't take
my eyes off it. I wondered how much it cost
and if my seamstress could copy it for me.

The prince and the girl danced and pranced.
My poor darlings were left prince-less.

A few days later, the prince made an announcement.
A glass slipper had been left at the castle. The prince
would marry the girl whose foot it fit. Our big chance!

After visiting every other mansion in the neighborhood,
the prince's valet arrived at our door.

"Me! Me!" said one of my darlings.

"No, me! Me!" said the other.

"One at a time," said the valet.

22

Each girl tried, but the shoe didn't fit.

Then Cindy pushed out a whisper.
"Please—let—me—try."

The shoe fit! Cindy pulled the match out of her pocket.

"Whaaaaaaat?" my darlings cried.

Cindy pushed out another whisper. She said something about a "pumpkin coach" and "mice that turned into horses." She even added a "fairy godmother." Please! There's no such thing!

But I still don't know where she got those shoes ...

A few days later, the prince married Cindy.
Poor man. He had no idea what he was getting
himself into. But *we* lived happily ever after!

THE END

OF COURSE YOU THINK THE GIANT WAS THE BAD GUY, TERRIFYING POOR LITTLE JACK. UNTIL NOW, YOU'VE HEARD ONLY JACK'S SIDE OF THE STORY. WELL, THE GIANT'S BEHIND THIS PAGE, AND HE'S READY TO SPILL THE BEANS ...

Trust Me, JACK'S BEANSTALK STINKS!

The Story of JACK AND THE BEANSTALK as Told by THE GIANT

by Eric Braun

illustrated by Cristian Bernardini

People think it's easy being a giant. You get to be rotten, grumpy, and loud. You're big and tough. You have gobs of treasure.

And nobody—**nobody**—tells you to behave.

Giant life is no picnic, though. It's hard to find shoes that fit. My knees hurt from the weight of my huge body. And I'm always hungry. *Always.*

But the worst thing? *Humans.*

Humans are part of a balanced giant breakfast.
But when you're not eating them, they're a real pain.
Sometimes they laugh at me behind my back. They call
me "stinky" and "fatso." They ring my doorbell and run
away. Ha ha ha, very funny!

31

This boy named Jack was extra bold. He came up through the clouds one day while I was out gathering a small breakfast. He tricked my wife into feeding him, then hid inside my house. I mean, come on. Would he hide inside a *human's* house? That's a crime!

Well, he didn't trick me. I could smell him.
(He smelled delicious.)

Maybe you still smell that Kiddie Kasserole from supper last night.

"FEE, FI, FO, FUM!"

I said. In Giant, this means something like
"Go on home now. I promise I won't eat you."

But he stayed in his hiding place, the little rat.

After breakfast I took a nap, like I always do.
Eating makes me tired. And when I did, Jack stole
a bag of gold!

Humans: nutritious *and* sneaky.

Some time later, Jack came back again. And again, he tricked my wife into letting him inside.

When I came home from picking up a light breakfast, I could smell him. I knew who it was.

Maybe you still smell that Little Dude Stew from supper last night.

101 DELICIOUS KID DISHES

"FEE, FI, FO, FUM!"

I yelled. This can also mean "Give me back my gold, and we'll call it even. I definitely won't eat you."

But he didn't come out.

Just like before, I ate my meal and tried to forget about Jack. I relaxed with my goose, the one that lays golden eggs. Soon I took a little snooze.

Of course that pesky boy couldn't let a guy rest. You know what he did?

HE *STOLE*
MY GOOSE,
THE LOUSY,
NO-GOOD,
MISERABLE THIEF!

The last time Jack came around, I called out,

"FEE, FI, FO, FUM!"

This can even mean "Darn it, I'm really angry now!"

My wife and I searched but couldn't find him. I kept looking, but soon I got hungry. (Big surprise.)

After breakfast, I enjoyed some lovely music.
My golden harp sang to me, and the sound
was even sweeter than boy-berry pie. I rested
my eyes a bit. I'd finally forgotten about Jack.

The next thing you know, my harp is calling, "Master! Master!" Jack was running off with it, and I thundered after. I almost caught up to them, too, but they disappeared into the clouds.

And there it was: a big beanstalk. Jack was climbing down it.

Well, I'm a smart guy. I know a dangerous thing when I see it. I didn't want to go down there. No way! But then my harp called out again.

So down I went. Down, down ...
That stalk was wobbly.
But I kept going.

The beanstalk shook once, twice, then toppled over. Jack had chopped it with an ax! I fell and broke my crown. That's an old-fashioned way of saying I whacked my head real good.

Even if you're a big, tough giant, that hurts.

My wife said I should forget about Jack. But sometimes I still look through the hole in the clouds.

Jack and his mother got rich selling golden eggs. They fattened up nicely. And Jack got married. My golden harp sang at the wedding. It was a lovely party.

I'll tell you one thing. Someday, when my crown feels better, I'm going down there to get my stuff back. Maybe I'll grab lunch while I'm there too.

THE END

OF COURSE YOU THINK THE PRINCE WAS A LOUSY, NO-GOOD GUY FOR BREAKING THE LITTLE MERMAID'S HEART. YOU NEVER HEARD HIS SIDE OF THE STORY. TURN THE PAGE, AND LET THE PRINCE TELL YOU HIMSELF ...

NO KIDDING, MERMAIDS ARE A JOKE!

The Story of THE LITTLE MERMAID as Told by THE PRINCE

by Nancy Loewen

illustrated by Amit Tayal

Are mermaids *real*?

A little while ago, I would have said NO WAY! Sea creatures with people faces and people arms but great big fish tails instead of legs? That's nuts!

Then I met this girl ...

My name is Prince Aleck. I'll admit, I'm sort of a practical joker. If you're looking for someone to put chili powder in the toothpaste, or to glue coins to sidewalks, I'm your guy.

But back to the girl ... I found her on the shore one morning, just lying there. She was wiggling her toes as if she'd never seen them before.

She couldn't talk, but she drew pictures in the sand.
They were pretty wild.

She drew a merman king on a throne ...

and a mean-looking sea witch ...

and a mermaid drinking a potion ...

and then she drew that same
mermaid girl, with human legs.

I was a little suspicious. Here's why:

Not long ago, I had a birthday party on my dad's ship. That night a terrible storm came up, and the ship broke apart. Everyone else got on a lifeboat, but the wind tossed me into the water. I had this weird dream that someone carried me through the water—someone with long, flowing hair ... and a tail.

Or was it a dream? I woke up the next morning on a distant beach. I didn't know how I'd gotten there.

Anyway, I made the mistake of telling my buddies. They've been teasing me ever since. I can't go for a swim without someone tossing a doll in the water. I have to check my oatmeal for fish scales.

"Did Dave put you up to this?" I asked the girl. "Or Jimmy? I bet it was Jimmy."

She looked confused.

Since I didn't know the girl's name, I called her Marlina, after the marlin, which is a big fish—get it? The problem was, I didn't know if I was dealing with a big fish TAIL or a big fish TALE.

I sure liked her, though. Everyone liked Marlina. She was great at charades. She could teach kids to swim and dive in no time.

And she blew us away at the local dance contest.

Still, I couldn't shake the feeling that my buddies were playing a trick on me. Especially when they said things like, "Your girlfriend's quite a catch" or "Aleck and Marlina, swimming in the sea,

K-I-S-S-I-N-G."

So I came up with a test.

Remember my birthday party? When I washed up on that beach? A girl from a nearby school had helped me out. She'd let me use her cell phone to call home. Her name was Kim. I texted her.

KIM

Want 2 B on TV?
B famous?
Got a deal for U.

...

I took Kim along to royal events. I drew hearts around her name in the sand. I wrote letters to her on fancy paper and sealed them with a kiss.

I sighed a lot and got really good at making goo-goo eyes.

I still hung out with Marlina. But I made it clear
we were just friends. "What a pal," I told her.

My parents were thrilled. "See, honey?" my mom said to my dad. "I told you he'd grow up sooner or later!"

This is what I expected to happen:

As soon as I was married, my friends, and Marlina, would admit that the mermaid thing was a joke. Then I would admit that I wasn't really married. The wedding was a fake! We'd have a good laugh, and life would go on as usual—or it would, once my parents got over being mad.

This is what *actually* happened:

I got fake-married. My friends gave me a nose-shaped pencil
sharpener and a case of chattering teeth as wedding gifts.

Marlina disappeared.

After the fake-wedding dance, for a split second, I thought I saw Marlina's face bobbing in the sea, far away. But when I blinked and looked again, all I saw was a bit of sea foam.

So, you tell me: Are mermaids real?

Don't tell anyone I said this, but my hunch is that they are.

THE END

OF COURSE YOU THINK GOLDILOCKS

WAS A BRAT WHO BROKE IN AND TRASHED THE THREE

BEARS' HOUSE. BUT THERE'S MORE TO THE STORY. AND

BABY BEAR IS READY TO SET THE RECORD STRAIGHT...

Believe Me, GOLDILOCKS ROCKS!

The Story of THE THREE BEARS
as Told by BABY BEAR

by **Nancy Loewen**
illustrated by **Tatevik Avakyan**

First things first: My name is NOT Baby Bear. It's Sam. And I am not nearly as wee or small or tiny as people think.

And Goldilocks? Ever since she broke into my house, she's been one of my best buddies. It's true that she takes a lot of chances. But she's not a bad kid—at least, no worse than me. Let me tell you the REAL story, and you'll see.

ME

GOLDIE

It all started when I complained about my breakfast. "Porridge AGAIN?" I said.

The next thing I knew, we were all out the door for a walk. Dad (also known as Papa Bear) grumbled something like, "He'll eat it if he's hungry enough."

At first I lagged behind.

"Stay where we can see you, Baby Bear!" called Mom (a.k.a. Mama Bear).

I ran ahead.

"Not so fast, Baby Bear!" called Dad.

I stamped my foot. "My NAME is SAM!" Then I ducked into the woods and took my secret shortcut home.

When I reached our house, I heard a voice. Someone was inside!

I didn't know what to do. Should I run to Mom and Dad for help? Or should I chase off the intruder myself?

BABY BEAR would have made a run for it. But not Sam.

I peeked through the kitchen window. A girl was taking pictures with her cell phone!

"Ha! This will teach Little Red Riding Hood to double-dare me," she muttered. "Goldilocks does not lose at Truth or Dare!"

She paused in front of the porridge bowls. "Eeeeeww," she said.

I liked her already.

Goldilocks took a picture of herself in my dad's chair ...

... then my mom's chair.

"You want proof, Little Miss Hoodie?" she asked. "Here it is!"

Next she took a picture of herself in my chair. When she got up, the chair stuck to her rear. She waddled around. She jumped up and down. Finally she gave the chair a good whack, and it came off—in pieces.

"Oops," she said. "There goes my allowance."

See? She meant to pay us back. Not that I cared—that chair was way too small for me too.

Upstairs, Goldilocks slipped off her shoes (which was very thoughtful of her) and took some video of herself jumping on my dad's bed. And my mom's bed.

"I can't believe I'm doing this!" she giggled.

Now, jumping on the beds is NOT ALLOWED in my house. This was my one and only chance to get away with it. I tapped at the window.

"ACK!"

Goldilocks shrieked.

"Let me in!" I begged. "I won't tell!"

Goldilocks opened the window, and we introduced ourselves. She apologized for breaking in. We were really quite civilized.

Then we **jumped** and **jumped** and **jumped** and **jumped** ...

82

... until we heard my mom calling from the woods. "Ba-by Bearrrr, where arrrre you?"

Goldilocks raised an eyebrow. "Baby Bear?" she asked. "Seriously?"

"Never mind!" I said. "Here's my plan ..."

I ran downstairs just as my parents were coming in.

"Baby Bear!" Mom exclaimed. "Thank goodness you're OK."

"There's an intruder upstairs!" I said.

"You know better than to go around making up stories," Dad said.

They sat down to eat their porridge—their cold, dried-out porridge.

I brought in my broken chair. "See? The intruder did this!"

"What a naughty thing to do!" Dad said. "Wrecking a perfectly good chair just to get our attention."

"But I SAW her!" I insisted. "Come on!"

I tugged them upstairs and showed them the messy covers on their beds.

"Baby Bear, you know that jumping on the beds is a big no-no!" Mom scolded.

"But the intruder—" I said, pushing them toward my room.

And as soon as we reached my bed ...

"BOO!"

Goldilocks yelled.

What happened next was priceless.

"Run!" Dad cried.

"To our safe place!" Mom screeched.
"And if we don't make it—I love you both with all my heart!"

I made sure they saw me chasing
Goldilocks through the woods. In between
her fake screams and my pretend growls,
we traded phone numbers.

Mom and Dad were so impressed with my courage that they gave me everything I asked for: a bigger chair, spicy breakfast burritos instead of porridge, and a promise to stop calling me Baby Bear.

Well, there was one thing I didn't get.

"Can't I jump on the beds? Just once in a while?" I asked.

"NO," my parents said. "ABSOLUTELY NOT."

Hey, it was worth a try.

THE END

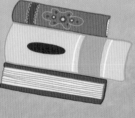

AND FINALLY ... THE STORY OF LITTLE RED RIDING HOOD

OF COURSE YOU THINK THE BIG BAD WOLF DID A HORRIBLE THING BY EATING LITTLE RED RIDING HOOD AND HER GRANNY. YOU DON'T KNOW THE OTHER SIDE OF THE STORY. TURN THE PAGE, AND HEAR WHAT THE WOLF HAS TO SAY...

Honestly, RED RIDING HOOD WAS ROTTEN!

The Story of LITTLE RED RIDING HOOD

as Told by THE WOLF

by **Trisha Speed Shaskan**   illustrated by **Gerald Guerlais**

Chomp! Chomp! Oh, I'm sorry. I was just finishing my lunch. My name's Wolf—Big Bad Wolf. You may have heard the story of Little Red Riding Hood. About a girl and her granny? Seems everyone has. My tail is different. Did I say *tail*? I meant *tale*.

eaten every last vegetable and fruit in the garden.
Every one.

Other wolves might've lunched on little forest
critters: chipmunks, bunnies, squirrels. But I'm
a vegetarian. That's right; I don't eat meat.
Well, I *try* not to. I **LOVE** apples. Honeycrisp,
Pink Lady, Golden Delicious ... Any kind,
really. But, sadly, it was a long time
until apple harvest.

I hadn't eaten in weeks. My stomach
growled and howled. It moaned and groaned.
It even roared. Then, my nose took over.

Sniff. Sniff. I took a whiff. What was it?

A girl.

Sniff. Sniff. I took a whiff. What was it?

Cake. Butter. In *this* forest? I had to investigate.

And there she was: Little Red Riding Hood. She looked as plump and juicy as a big, sweet APPLE.

Little Red waved her cape. "Isn't it pretty?" she said.

"Yeah," I said.

"Aren't I pretty?" she said.

Was she admiring herself in that puddle?

"With this cape," she said, "I'm even prettier than usual."

Boy, someone sure was full of herself. My stomach growled.

Little Red twirled a strand of hair. "Mother says the cape looks grand with my skin. My skin shines likes pearls."

Or the meat of a ripe apple, I thought, licking my chops.

Remember, I hadn't eaten in weeks.

Time to chomp!

But then Little Red said, "I can't wait until Granny sees how pretty I am today. I'm bringing her cake and butter from my mother."

My stomach howled. TWO meals, I thought: Granny for breakfast, Little Red for lunch (and cake and butter for dessert).

"Where does Granny live?" I asked.

Little Red pointed. "Down there, in the clearing. The brown house."

I knew that house. And I had a plan.

"Let's play a game," I said.

Little Red smiled. "I'm awesome at games."

"I bet you are," I said. "You take this path. I'll take that path. And let's see who arrives at Granny's first."

"I will," she said. "I'm the prettiest *and* the fastest."

"I bet you are," I said.

My stomach moaned. Before it groaned, I ran. No one knows the forest like I do. I chose the shorter path.

Sniff. Sniff. I took a whiff. What was it?

Apple air freshener?

Tap, tap. I knocked on the door.

"Who's there?" called out a voice.

"Your granddaughter," I squeaked. "I've brought you cake and butter from Mother."

"Door's open," Granny said.

Granny tugged at her nightcap. "Green,"
she said. "Isn't it pretty?"

Pretty like a Granny Smith apple, I thought.

"Aren't I pretty?" Granny said.

You must've heard the saying "the apple
doesn't fall far from the tree"? Well, it's true.

My stomach roared.

"What's that noise?" Granny asked.

Chomp! Chomp!

I *had* to eat her. She was no
McIntosh apple, but not too bad.

I still felt hungry.

Tap, tap. Little Red knocked on the door.

"Who's there?" I called out, crawling into Granny's bed.

"Your granddaughter," Little Red said. "I've brought you cake and butter from Mother."

"Door's open," I said.

Little Red walked in and caught a glimpse of herself in the mirror. "Isn't my cape pretty, Granny?" she said. "Aren't I pretty?"

I clenched my teeth.

"**Granny,**" Little Red said,
"what deep dark eyes I have."

"**Mmmhmm,**" I said,
"the color of apple seeds."

"**Granny,**" she said,
"what perfect ears I have."

"**Mmmhmm,**" I said,
"shaped like sharply cut apple slices."

"**Granny,**" *she said,*
"what pretty red lips I have."

"**Mmmhmm,**" I said, "Red Delicious."

"**Granny,**" *she said,*
"what lovely skin I have."

Chomp! Chomp!

I ate her up. What can I say? Things look different when you're hungry. She was no Fuji or Crispin apple (in fact, to be honest, she was a bit rotten), but she was better than nothing.

Plus, I got dessert.

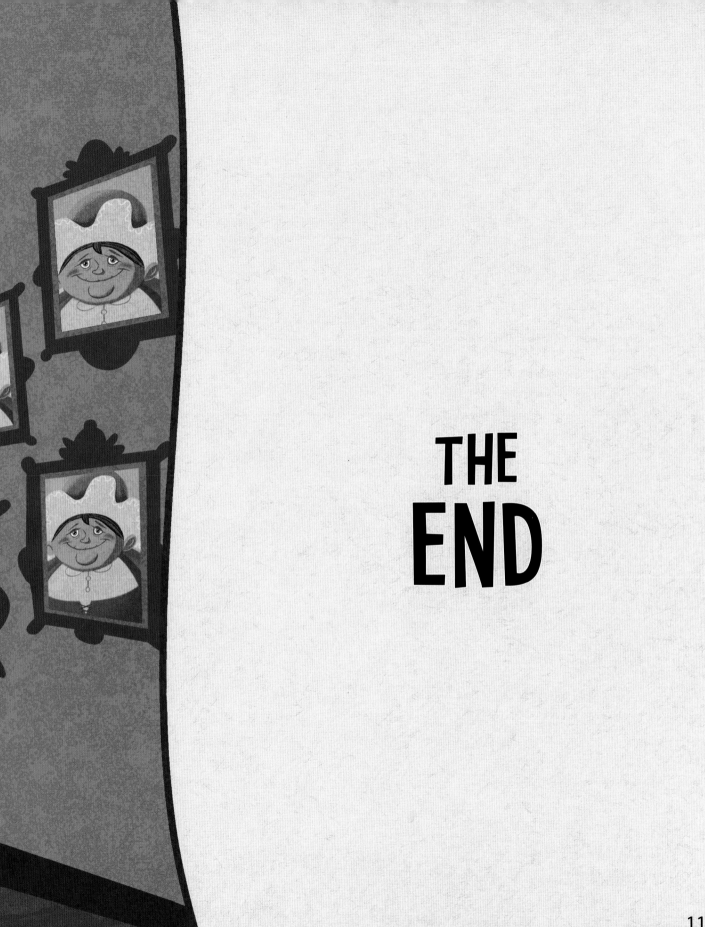

THE
END

Think About It

THE STORY OF CINDERELLA AS TOLD BY THE WICKED STEPMOTHER

If you could be one of the main characters in this version of *Cinderella*, who would you be, and why? The stepmother or one of the stepsisters? Cinderella? The prince?

THE STORY OF JACK AND THE BEANSTALK AS TOLD BY THE GIANT

The giant says it's hard to be a giant. Humans bother him, and he just wants to be left alone. Do you believe him? Why or why not?

THE STORY OF THE LITTLE MERMAID AS TOLD BY THE PRINCE

If Marlina told the story instead of the prince, what details might she tell differently? What if Kim told the story from her point of view?

THE STORY OF THE THREE BEARS AS TOLD BY BABY BEAR

Read a classic version of *Goldilocks and the Three Bears* and compare it to Sam's version. What are some things that happen in this story that don't happen in the classic? What are some things that happen in the classic story that don't appear in this one?

THE STORY OF LITTLE RED RIDING HOOD AS TOLD BY THE WOLF

If it had been apple season, do you think Wolf would've eaten Little Red and her grandma? Why or why not?

HUNGRY FOR MORE?
GET A SECOND HELPING!

ANOTHER OTHER SIDE OF THE STORY:
FAIRY TALES WITH A TWIST

BEAUTY AND THE BEAST

SNOW WHITE

RAPUNZEL

SLEEPING BEAUTY

THE FROG PRINCE

AUTHORS AND ILLUSTRATORS

ERIC BRAUN

Eric Braun writes fiction and nonfiction for kids, teens, and adults, but sometimes he still dreams of being a professional skateboarder. He is a 2013 McKnight Fellow and also a nice fellow. He lives in Minneapolis with his wife, sons, and gecko. Learn more at www.heyericbraun.com.

NANCY LOEWEN

Nancy Loewen has published more than 100 books for children. Recent awards include: 2013 Oppenheim Toy Portfolio Best Book Award (*Baby Wants Mama*); 2012 Minnesota Book Awards finalist (*The LAST Day of Kindergarten*); and 2010 AEP Distinguished Achievement Award (*Writer's Toolbox series*). She's also received awards from the American Library Association and the New York Public Library. Nancy lives in the Twin Cities and holds an MFA in Creative Writing from Hamline University, St. Paul. She likes to read, garden, cook, walk her dog, and collect weird figurines from thrift stores.

TRISHA SPEED SHASKAN

Trisha Speed Shaskan has written more than 40 books for children. She was a recipient of a 2012 Minnesota State Artist's Initiative Grant and won the 2009 McKnight Artist Fellowship for Writers, Loft Award in Children's Literature/Older Children. Trisha received her MFA in Creative Writing from Minnesota State University, Mankato. She works as a literacy coordinator for an after-school program and teaches youth writing classes at The Loft Literary Center. Trisha lives with her husband, children's book author and illustrator Stephen Shaskan, and their cat, Eartha, in Minneapolis.

TATEVIK AVAKYAN

Tatevik Avakyan has illustrated many books for children and tweens, which, as it turns out, are her absolute favorite subjects! She always loved drawing as a child and knew she wanted to be an illustrator as early as her teens. She later earned her degree from California State University of Northridge. Tatevik currently lives and works in Southern California with her husband and son.

CRISTIAN BERNARDINI

Born in Buenos Aires, Argentina, in 1975, Cristian Bernardini is a graphic designer and a graduate of the University of Buenos Aires. Currently Cristian does design work and illustration for various studios and publishers, as well as developments in the field of animation for both TV media and media in general.

GERALD GUERLAIS

Born in Nantes, France, Gerald Guerlais grew up in nine cities, wearing as many different shoes as his shoeseller parents sold. He graduated in 1998 from the National School of Applied Art (Olivier de Serres) and honed his craft at a web design company, an event studio, a video-games studio, and several animation studios. Aside from his work as an illustrator, Gerald manages the French Comics Artists Association "Rendez-Vous" and co-leads (with Japanese artist Daisuke Tsutsumi) the artistic and charity project "Sketchtravel," a real sketchbook shared by 70 illustrators from all around the world.

AMIT TAYAL

Amit Tayal is an award-winning illustrator. Working for almost a decade, Amit has produced a wide range of illustration styles, using both digital and traditional methods. Amit has worked at various publications and animation studios. His work has appeared in educational, children's, and comic books around the world and has won multiple awards.

Special thanks to our adviser, Terry Flaherty, PhD, Professor of English,
Minnesota State University, Mankato, for his expertise.

Editor: Jill Kalz
Designer: Lori Bye
Art Director: Nathan Gassman
Production Specialist: Kathy McColley
The illustrations in this book were created digitally.

Design elements: Shutterstock

Picture Window Books are published by Capstone,
1710 Roe Crest Drive, North Mankato, Minnesota 56003
www.capstonepub.com

Library of Congress Cataloging-in-Publication Data
Braun, Eric, 1971–
  The other side of the story : fairy tales with a twist / by Eric Braun,
Nancy Loewen, and Trisha Speed Shaskan ; illustrated by Tatevik Avakyan,
Gerald Guerlais, Amit Tayal, Cristian Bernardini.
       pages cm.—(Nonfiction picture books. the other side of the story.)
  Summary: "Introduces the concept of point of view through retellings of five
classic fairy tales - 'Cinderella,' 'Jack and the Beanstalk,' 'The Little Mermaid,'
'Goldilocks and the Three Bears,' and 'Little Red Riding Hood' - by the stories'
supporting characters"—Provided by publisher.
  ISBN 978-1-4795-5697-7 (paper over board)
1. Fairy tales—History and criticism. I. Title.

  GR550.B656 2014
  398.2—dc23   2013046718

Printed in China.
022015   008771